earthling

stories

doris w. cheng

word west press | brooklyn, new york

isbn: 978-1-7369477-6-0

published by word west in brooklyn, ny

first us edition 2021

printed in the usa

www.wordwest.co

cover & interior design: word west

For my family. You know who you are.

table of contents

hereafter

People will say anything at a funeral. Take the Reverend Griggs. He hands me a tissue and says, "There, there, don't cry. Your mother is always with you, even in the Hereafter."

I sigh. "I wish, Reverend. There's something I meant to ask her." I blow my nose. "But we both saw that ebony wood casket—my six-thousand-dollar last effort to please—disappear into the ground. Wherever she is now, it's not with me."

Later that night, I am watching *The Joy Luck Club* when my mother climbs out of her grave and stands at my bedside. The clock says three AM. Richard snores loudly next to me. "Doris," she says, "Did you really pay six thousand dollars for an ebony wood casket? And upgrade my burial plot to the 'deluxe water view'? My God, you are wasteful!"

Although she is semi-transparent and waxy from the embalming fluid, she looks surprisingly good. I put out my hand and it passes right through her midsection. She swats it away. "Don't."

I nearly drop the remote. Sitting up, I ask her what it's like in the Hereafter. She begins to change shape, turning into a mule, a mouse, then a turtle with a hard scabbed shell.

"Hmph," she says after she changes back to herself, "It's great. The cherubs fight to hold my hand. The angels give me harp solos because I'm the only one who can do glissandos. All the souls ask me for advice. Something you might have tried doing once in a while."

I roll my eyes. I can guess what's coming next. "Think—" She pauses. "It's not too late to give up writing and go into pharmaceuticals."

She is the same as ever. Still, I decide to tell her what's been bothering me. Mothers, I say, are supposed to provide closure before they die. They are supposed to tell their daughters they're proud of them—tell them they love them. That's what happens in the *The Joy Luck Club*. I clear my throat and give her a nudging look. Perhaps there is something she forgot to tell me before she died? Something she would like to tell me now?

As usual, she isn't listening. She swishes her arms and flickers with a murky light, like a firefly at the bottom of a pond. "Get up," she says. "We're going to cut coupons."

No way. I slump under the covers. Then I brighten—maybe we'll have a heart-to-heart over coupons. That's something else that happens in *The Joy Luck Club*.

So I get up, follow her to the kitchen, and dig through the recycling bin for circulars. My mother floats around the table, pointing out the extra good deals and remarking on my sloppy use of scissors. She says, "Idiot, why buy a Starbucks latte every day? That's one thousand eight hundred twenty-five dollars you could be saving in one year! Which will come in handy when Richard dumps you because of your cooking."

I throw down the scissors. Looking at the clock, I pointedly suggest it must be time for her to be getting back to the Hereafter, it being so wonderful and all. Besides, her angel friends were probably looking for her. "Right," she says, "They miss me terribly when I'm gone. They weep deluges. But it's your fault. I wouldn't have come back at all if you weren't so useless."

That steams me. I grab the coupons and throw them into the garbage. I'm about to go back to bed, slamming the door behind me like a fractious teenager, when she transforms again, into a sparrow, a nestling flapping helplessly on the kitchen floor.

When she becomes herself again she is crying. "I hate the Hereafter. I'm so lonely. God says I'm controlling and narcissistic and that's why none of the other souls want to be my friend. That God is a know-nothing loser." Her angry tears dissolve into vapor.

I have never seen my mother cry before. She grows smaller, dimmer, and soon she is a nothing more than a wisp glistening wetly on the linoleum. In a minute she'll be gone forever. I fish the coupons out of the garbage and stack them in a pile. I stumble to my knees. "Don't cry, Mom. I'll always be with you," I say.

Now she is nothing more than rippled air, the intake of breath after a sigh. Before it's too late, I reach out for what particles of her I can find.

self-reflection

Someone has left a present on my doorstep. There's no card, no occasion I can think of, but my daughter is excited to open it so I bring it inside. Turns out it's a stuffed bear. It's cute except for the fact that it won't stop talking. It says things to my daughter like "Take only one cookie, Sweetie" or "No more than thirty minutes of TV. Wooden puzzles are more fun, don't you think?"

When I pick him up for a closer look, the bear cocks his sailor-hatted head at me. "Doris," he says. "All that dirty laundry hosts harmful bacteria. And the mold in your refrigerator—it's a miracle no one has gotten salmonella."

I want to throw the bear in the garbage. But I consult my parenting book to make sure. The book says that under no circumstance am I to throw the bear in the garbage. Children, it says, must learn to appreciate the gifts they are given. "Living with the bear will teach your child habits of gratitude and self-reflection."

Of course I want to do the right thing as a parent. But it's hard to live with the bear. The bear has many demands, among them that I give my daughter only organic snacks and play Mozart in the car. He also likes to correct my spelling and point out better ways to organize my drawers.

One night my daughter and I watch the Miss America pageant. The bear perches on the back of the sofa and makes snide comments in my ear. "This show perpetuates the objectification of women. As the mother of a girl, you are setting a terrible example."

"But it's a scholarship competition!" I sputter. "We like the pretty dresses!"

"You should be enriching your daughter at this formative stage of her life." He purses his furry lips. "There is nothing intellectually or spiritually redeeming about this spectacle. How about some *Baywatch* while you're at it?" The bear doesn't shut up until I change the channel to PBS.

My daughter is a compliant soul. She nods when the bear insists on "fixing" her homework before she turns it in. She says nothing when he asks, after a pointed pause, is she really sure she wants to wear the red tights with the pink dress? It's not until she wakes up one night to find him gazing at her with unblinking plastic eyes that she begins to crack.

"Mom," she whispers, "I don't like how Teddy is always watching me." She clutches me tightly, a passenger on a sinking ship.

She starts to wash her hands until they're raw. She picks up objects around the house—the newspaper, a hairbrush—and sniffs them, wanting to know if smells can make a person sick. The sight of my beautiful girl sniffing a spatula sends me from the room weeping.

The bear finds me ironing. He tells me to stop crying. He says I need to work on my gratitude and self-reflection, and besides, I am getting tears and snot all over the clean laundry. I cry harder.

When my daughter refuses to hug me unless she is wearing oven mitts, I clench my teeth. I see she is wrapped in an invisible cocoon. I want to dig my nails into the sticky threads, rip them away before she transforms into something unrecognizable. It's time to stop crying.

I invite the bear to join us on a picnic in the woods. I bring a basket of nitrate-filled lunchmeat and partially hydrogenated cookies. While he is busy lecturing us about the dangers of processed foods, we book it to the car. We tumble in and lock the doors. I switch on the ignition.

I can hear him yelling. His voice is insistent, close. "Come back! You're doing everything wrong! You'll never get her into Harvard!"

My daughter plugs her ears. I slam the car into reverse and feel a soft thump. I drive over the bear, forward and back, forward and back, until I no longer hear his voice.

cain, knocking

My brother is a superstar. Dad says I could learn a thing or two from him. He says if I stop giving every sad sack I meet a hand-carved spoon, who knows, I might become Assistant Sales Coordinator one day like Dale. (Unlikely, he admits, but at the very least I should fill out the application to sort mail at Dale's company.)

Still, I open the door when a stranger knocks.

It's a hairy guy wearing nothing but a loincloth.

I figure he's a Jehovah's Witness so I invite him in to help him make his quota. I put down my chisel. "I'm Carl," I say.

But he doesn't have any pamphlets. He stomps around my living room and knocks over the walking stick I'm carving. He punches himself in the forehead. "Why does Father overlook the fruits of my labor? Why does He regard only my brother's offerings?"

I feel for the guy. He's got a superstar brother too. I bring him a wooden spoon and a cup of tea to go with it but he throws them to the floor.

I mop up the tea. I give him advice: "My shrink says no family is perfect. He says it's important to practice 'loving forbearance.'" I explain it's like when Dad tells me not to come over on Fathers Day because he's getting a steak dinner with Dale and I say "sure thing" and microwave a pizza.

The guy blinks, then leaves.

He comes back the next day even more distraught. "Father denigrated my sheaves of wheat! Yet He rejoiced in my brother's lamb."

I make soothing noises. I tell him parents have a lot on their minds nowadays and sometimes, they forget things. Like last year when I carved a beautiful swan for my dad's birthday. It had fine-gouged feathers and a neck that rippled like water. But Dad got so distracted by the iPhone Dale gave him that he tossed out the swan with the recycling. "My shrink says—"

"Father paraded my brother's offering far and wide, though my brother did deceive Him with his sickliest animal. My sheaves he left for the birds." The guy picks up a vase and throws it at the wall.

"My shrink says, uh..." I stop. I am remembering how long it took me to dig the swan out of the dumpster. When I finally found it under a wad of poopie diapers, its neck had snapped clean off. Without it the body looked like it could have belonged to any old duck.

The guy tries to pick up the TV but it's too heavy. I help him and together we throw it out the window. My fingers tingle as I watch the plastic cube explode into pieces on the pavement.

"And my brother? Mirthful." The guy makes a fist and slaps it against his palm. "He must be reckoned with."

"I'll come with you," I offer. I figure he needs the moral support.

The next day we wait in an empty field. I whittle the handle of my walking stick. The guy's brother is a no-show. After a couple hours my father walks by on his way to play golf with Dale. His lip curls when he sees me. "For Christ's sake, Carl, why are you standing in an empty field with this goober? I bet you didn't fill out that job application like I told you to!" He grabs my ear and yanks it from side to side. My head rolls like it's about to come off my body.

The hairy guy smacks my father's hand away. My father gives me a look. He doesn't say a word. His expression sinks into me like a hammer to the bottom of a pond.

After my father leaves I jab the guy in the chest. "What the heck? Remember what I told you—what my shrink said?" My fingers tingle.

"You're a fool," he says. He laughs.

The next thing I know I'm holding the walking stick like a sword. I whack the guy in the head. I whack him again and again until he shudders and his hair puffs out like feathers. I blink and suddenly he is a starling. He scratches, shrieks, and flies away. Black feathers float to the ground like ash.

The sky darkens. I hear tiny hiccupping sounds and realize they are coming from deep inside my chest.

"Hello?" I say to the empty field. There is no reply.

I press my walking stick into the earth and lurch forward. I take one step, then another. I want my father.

parcel post

There once lived a woman who kept her baby in a box.

She worked as a letter sorter at the post office and kept the box at her feet. Her parents died when she was young, leaving her with nothing but debt, and after a solitary upbringing, she found solace in her work and in her baby. Not one to gossip or flirt, she was able to sort the mail with one hand and tickle the baby's chin or check her diaper with the other. Even when her mind was occupied with distribution routes and sorting codes, her hands remembered what needed to be done. "A machine," her supervisor said with a shake of his head. The baby was of a calm disposition and amused herself until the end of the day. Then the woman checked the mailbags for stray letters, scooped up her child, swaddled her, and took her home.

The holidays were approaching, and the woman had been given the task of sorting illegibly addressed letters, work that no one else cared to do.

She enjoyed the constancy of the mail; she took pride in correcting errors and directing letters to their rightful destination. But on the Friday before Christmas, she arrived at the post office late. The baby had a cold, was cutting a tooth on top of that, and the woman had paced the floor of her apartment all night, patting the baby's back and giving her cold cloths to suck. She saw the newspaper on her desk as she was putting away her coat. Its headline seemed to confirm the rumors she had heard whispered around the office for weeks: GOVERNMENT TO AUTOMATE ALL POSTAL FUNCTIONS; THOUSANDS OF LAYOFFS EXPECTED. She put the newspaper in the wastebasket.

She unwrapped the baby as usual, but the child was irritable. Every time the woman tried to settle her in the box, the baby cried and clutched at her sleeves. At first the woman made soothing sounds, then she tried to distract her with a rattle. Finally, she lost patience and began to speak sternly, as if to a subordinate: "Enough tomfoolery. Mama needs to work. Do you understand?"

The janitress laughed gleefully. An old woman so arthritic she sometimes spent entire days cleaning one corner of the building, she had been sweeping behind the sorting room door.

"That cake ain't worth the candle, ha ha! You're better off talking to a houseplant." She had never approved of the woman having a baby alone, with no parents, no man in the picture, and took every opportunity to say so (even though she herself was considered odd by many). Now she stopped to shake her broom at the woman.

"What could the likes of you know about mothering?"

Normally the woman ignored comments like these. She pitied the janitress who, like herself, had no family or friends. This morning, however, she snapped, "Be quiet! I know what I'm doing, for God's sake. Go back to your work."

The janitress turned back to her sweeping. Shuffling away, she muttered, "Elle crève dans sapeau."

The woman rummaged through her purse and found a piece of chocolate. The child took it, whimpering, and the woman picked up a batch of letters and began separating them into piles. Despite her weariness, the woman's hands moved rapidly, grabbing letters, tossing them into a pigeonholed mail sorter. But the baby didn't sleep. She had a cough that woke her every time she closed her eyes, and after a while, this made the baby cry. Each time she cried, the woman held her to her breast with one hand and continued sorting mail with the other.

Her supervisor walked over as she started on the second mailbag. He was a peacock of a man and liked to think his female coworkers were secretly in love with him. Every so often, he tried to discover the identity of the baby's father but was never successful. He leaned an elbow on her desk and pretended not to notice the baby.

"I've never seen so much mail," he said. "With the world going down the tubes, people seem to think the only thing they can count on is mail delivery."

"You can say that again," she said. She did not look up nor did her hands stop their constant motion, flying back and forth like a pair of nesting birds. She considered asking whether he knew anything about the layoffs. But she did not want to encourage further conversation, so she said nothing. In truth, she despised the supervisor. Jobs were scarce so she was careful to hide her feelings.

The supervisor took her reserve for receptiveness and complimented her hair. He spoke of a French restaurant in town, how he was certain she would enjoy its air of refinement, and he proposed that she dine with him that evening. One has not lived, he declared, one has not experienced all that life has to offer, until one has tasted ris de veaux.

The woman found his self-regard insufferable. She had excused herself from his advances on other occasions, and she now pleaded fatigue. She was coming down with a cold. She would not want him to catch it.

The supervisor thought she was being coy. "La, it would be an honor to catch any cold of yours!" he said with false gallantry.

The baby fussed, and the woman stopped to pat her. She saw that the second mailbag was still almost full—she was falling behind. With more firmness now, she refused the supervisor again. "Awfully nice of you to think of me, but I can't do it. Thanks anyway." She pointedly turned back to her work, but he did not leave her desk. He continued to press her until he was summoned by a phone call.

When the supervisor had gone, the woman put the baby back in the box. Almost at once the child began to howl. A clerk from the front office poked her head through the doorway. The noise, she said, was disturbing the customers—mightn't the woman find a way to control her child? The woman nodded, but when the clerk disappeared, she let out an oath. She picked up the baby and began to pace the room, bouncing her up and down like a pony ride at the fair. Every once in a while she stopped to sort a few letters. It was taking longer than usual to determine the course of each letter; she required extra disconcerting seconds to tell the difference between a 1 and a 7, or a D and an O. Her arms burned from holding the baby on one side and sorting mail with the other.

The baby continued to cry and the woman carried her into the hallway. She passed two men, both letter carriers, leaning against the wall smoking and overheard one say to the other, "I'm suffocating here. I would take the layoff, but I'm still paying for my wife's new teeth. Only three molars to go."

She walked into the break room. The supervisor was drinking coffee and eating a Turkish Delight. "Ah, we have to stop meeting like this!" he said when he saw her, smiling so widely he showed his gums.

"Yes, we must," she said. She spun on her heel and left. She shifted the baby from one arm to the other. She remembered a fishmonger in her village who had a tumor growing from her side. It started out as an extra envelope of flesh, no bigger than three fingers, but it continued to grow and eventually it reached the size of a melon. The fishmonger used to carry the tumor in a sling when she brought her fish to market.

Back at her desk, the woman looked around. She never left for the day until she had completed every task. Piles of letters covered the surface of her desk. Bags of mail ringed the room. Each wail cranked a winch that wound her tighter and tighter. She put the baby in the box, scooped a pile of mail from the bag, and began to sort. If she wasn't brought any additional bags, she ought to be able to get through it all.

The janitress walked by pushing a broom. She looked at the woman and smiled slyly. Seeing her, the woman quickly picked the baby up again. She made a show of rocking her child. She patted her back—gently at first, then harder, as if to startle her into silence—but the cries only came faster, an avalanche of woe.

The phone rang. It was the delivery coordinator, calling to see if she had finished the second mailbag. The trucks were preparing their routes, he said, and he wanted to get as many letters out for delivery as possible.

The woman told him not yet. She had to shout over the crying and wasn't sure if he could hear her. He said, "Oh, and one more thing. The boss wants to know if you've reconsidered dinner tonight—" She clapped the phone back in its cradle.

The woman closed her eyes. She remembered a tomcat that used to roam her neighborhood when she was a child, a monstrous black and white animal that yowled from dusk to dawn. She remembered how quiet it became after someone left out a dish of poisoned tuna.

Holding the baby, she stood at the window. She pushed the child to the glass and looked out at the sidewalk, the holiday shoppers laden with purchases. They were too far away to hear the sound of crying, or anything else that might happen, inside the post office. She patted the baby, gave her a rough vigorous shake. "Quiet, you! Why can't you just be quiet?" She dropped the baby back in the box and resolved to let her cry, no matter what.

The child shrieked. Her face grew swollen, her legs stabbed the air with sharp, jerky motions. The woman jammed the box under her desk as far as it would go and picked up a handful of mail. She found it difficult to work at first. The sound of crying was a sea surge pounding at her brain. If she did not buttress herself, it would swallow her. She kept her hands moving, back and forth, back and forth, and after some time, she found a rhythm beneath the noise. She slipped into an unthinking flow. Her hands took on a mind of their own, and letters flew through the air like magician's knives. Mailbags opened and closed, carts rolled from one side of the room to the other. The baby's screaming receded. The woman retreated to a room inside her mind: She worked at her desk but was no longer the manual operator of her body. She was very far away. When she reached the bottom of the last mailbag, it was evening.

The woman's breasts ached and she noticed a damp trickle down her front. How long had it been since she fed the baby? She looked under her desk. The baby and the box were gone.

She stared for a moment in disbelief. Then she knelt to look more closely. The baby was not yet crawling—she couldn't have gone far. Peering into the corner, she saw only her lunch box and a pair of worn slippers.

Panicked, she threw open her desk drawers.

She dumped packages out of bins and plunged her hands into mail cubbies. She overturned boxes of bulk mail. She saw a group of co-workers by the door. Pushing herself into the middle of their chatter, she tugged at their sleeves—surely they had seen her baby? They had always considered her standoffish, the subject of gossip and judgment. Now they stepped back in alarm, as if stumbling upon a crime scene. Some shook their heads. A few suggested calling the police. No one had seen anything.

The woman ran into the central processing room. She found the supervisor at his desk picking his teeth. "Where is my baby?" she demanded.

He was surprised by her question. She had never approached him so directly. Her appearance alarmed him—eyes wide, mouth a circle of shock, as if she had gazed upon a basilisk. The hair he complimented earlier flew wildly about her face. "Now, now," he said. "You need to calm down. Have you seen yourself? You look a fright."

"My baby's missing. Somebody needs to do something!"

"Try the Lost and Found. The post office is not in the habit of losing things."

"Are you kidding me?"

"Huh! Well, no need to worry, she'll turn up eventually. Children often wander off." He began to pack up his briefcase. "I'm sure you'll be more careful next time."

The woman found his condescension intolerable. A thought occurred to her. "Was it you? Did you think you could get me to go to dinner if you got rid of her? Tell me!"

He looked at her coldly. "That is ridiculous. There is no shortage of women who want to spend time with me. Rest assured I have found another companion for dinner this evening." He put on his overcoat and left.

The woman ran through the building. She checked every room—administrative offices, closets, even the basement incinerator, where she paused for a moment to listen to the moaning of the flames. It came to her that the janitress might have seen something. The old woman was always lurking in corners, listening to every conversation, watching every movement. The woman found her behind the supervisor's door, sweeping dirt from one side of the floor to the other.

"My baby's gone. Have you seen her?"

"What's that?" The old woman turned to her slowly.

She really should have retired long ago, but she was poor and had no other income. Besides, she enjoyed coming to work every day and observing the rivalries, the little workplace dramas. There was also the fact that after working at the post office for so many years, she had collected enough secrets to make everyone afraid of her.

"Look, I know you spy on everyone all day long. You know where she is. Don't pretend."

The janitress sniffed. "What kind of mother loses her child? I'm not going to tell you anything. Remember how you told me to be quiet? Well, why should I talk now, just because you say so?" She smacked her lips, enjoying herself.

The woman was frantic. She clasped her hands and begged. "Please. If you know anything, you've got to tell me. I need your help."

"Remember how you said you knew what you were doing? Ha, ha, ça, c'est drôle! Maybe you're not better than everyone else." The janitress pointed a bony finger squarely at the woman's forehead. "Maybe you're care-less and sloppy."

The woman recoiled. In that moment, she hated the janitress. She wondered if the old woman was a witch—if she had placed some kind of curse on her. But was there any curse worse than losing your child? She lunged. She grabbed the janitress by the wrist and dug her nails into her skin. "I've had enough of your bunk, you old crone! You better tell me where my baby is."

The janitress shrank. She tried to yank her wrist back, but the woman held fast. "Come on, leave me alone," she whined. "I was just having some fun with you. I don't know anything. How should I know where your baby is?"

Seeing the janitress cower before her, the woman felt only fury. A door inside of her, clamped shut all her life, flung open. She shoved the janitress in the chest. "You nasty, nasty hag. No one can stand you. That's the reason you're alone in the world." She put her face close to the janitress, so close she could see every pockmark and smell her whiskey breath. She saw fear darting in the old woman's eyes like a lamprey. She slapped her. "You smell like rotten meat. You disgust me."

The janitress cried, "Stop! Stop! You're hurting me."

But the woman ignored her cries. She rained blow after blow upon the old woman until the janitress fell to the floor. Then she knelt over her. "Go home or don't. It doesn't matter. No one cares whether you live or die."

The woman left the post office. She visited the police station, where she filled out a report. She checked the hospitals to see if anyone had brought in an unnamed baby. Then she went home and collapsed in her bed. Her knuckles were bruised, and she cradled her hand against her chest. Where before her baby's face had appeared every time she closed her eyes, she now saw only the janitress, bleeding and bloated beyond recognition.

Early the next morning, the woman's mail arrived. Among the holiday cards and coupon flyers was a familiar-looking box, addressed in what appeared to be her own handwriting. She tore open the box. Inside was her baby, pale and still. She swayed in disbelief and quickly scooped up her child. She patted the baby's cheeks, put breast milk in her mouth. She held her close until she felt the child move, finally, against her body.

corner of my eye

I saw Meredith at breakfast today. It had been two, maybe three years since I'd seen her—really looked at her, that is. She usually resided in my peripheral vision, like a dust mote floating in the corner of my eye.

"Hi, Mom," she said.

I was overcome. I loved my girl so much. "Honey, how did you sleep? How are things at school? Tell me everything." I noticed her hair was in a complicated French braid; she must have learned to do that on her own.

She proceeded to tell me all about a fifth-grade project that involved toothpicks and copper wire and teeny tiny robots. There was some sort of classroom drama. I tried to pay attention. But I was packing her little sisters' lunches and trying to remember who needed to bring their violin and who needed to return their library book. The dog tipped over the garbage pail and I had to wrestle a chicken bone from its mouth. I know I missed some details. But I thought, thank God I never have to worry about Meredith.

Around then Hallie's anxiety got so bad she began levitating. I had to meet with the principal and child psychologist and drive her to a social skills group twice a week so she could play board games and practice keeping both feet on the ground. On top of that Fiona developed amblyopia. Her left eye starting rolling around in her head like a greasy marble in a ball socket. When I wasn't driving Hallie to therapy I was on the Internet researching "levitation treatment" and "child has loose eyeball."

Some time later I ran into Meredith in the kitchen. I'd come in to fix myself a cup of tea and saw her peering into the refrigerator.

"What's going on, sweetie?" I was happy she was there. I hadn't seen her in a while, though I knew she was around. I could tell she'd gotten taller and more womanly.

"Nothing much. Everything's fine." She closed the fridge door. "We're out of yogurt."

"Sorry. I've been so busy I haven't had time to get to the store. Your sisters, their appointments—"

She told me it was no biggie. She was understanding, full of grace. I told her I was grateful to have an independent and resourceful daughter who always did what was expected of her. I hugged her.

I'm kind of fuzzy on Meredith's high school years. I remember her little sisters were putting me through the wringer. Hallie needed gravitational therapy, which meant I had to tie cans of soup to her feet every night and force her into a heavy-footed walk. Fiona's doctor recommended she get a mechanical eye. I was buried in insurance paperwork and probably a little depressed. I think Meredith played field hockey. Or maybe it was lacrosse. I vaguely recall there being a stick of some sort.

Whatever it was, I'm sure she did well because she's a team player. Other kids might drink at parties and throw up on people's lawns, but not her. She's too considerate for that.

I passed her on the stairs from time to time. Each time she was more self-possessed than the last. Sometimes I felt a hand reach its way inside me and strum a high minor chord along my rib cage. The note reverberated in my chest cavity.

The last time I saw her was in the spring of her senior year. Or maybe she had already graduated, I can't say for sure. I woke up, looked out the window, and saw her in the yard tending a roaring flame. She was inflating a hot air balloon.

I ran downstairs. By the time I got outside she was already in the basket. The balloon began to float upward.

"Come down, Meredith!" I told her she had to let me know where she was going. She wasn't licensed and besides, she would need a warmer jacket if she was going to spend time in the stratosphere.

Meredith untied the ropes. She tossed out some ballast and the balloon began to climb. I shouted at her to be careful. I wanted her to know that a mother's love is infinite, but I wasn't sure if she could hear me at that point.

She waved. The balloon crested the tree line and found an air current. A sudden gust took it up and away. I couldn't tell if she was smiling. She kept waving until she was just a dot on the horizon, no bigger than a dust mote. The dog started barking and I turned to shush it. When I looked forher again she was gone.

adverse possession

I am floating on a mountaintop. The sky is a pillowy blue, and a choir of seraphim sings "It Is Well With My Soul" in diatonic harmony. Below, my body lies in the ICU amid tubes and wires and machines. My organs are collapsing from septic shock.

God shows up as a flaming chicken. "Doris," He says, shaking his tail feathers, "Cut the crap."

"Huh?" I sputter. I momentarily lose altitude. "What did I do?"

He enumerates my sins one fiery talon at a time. "Yelling at your kids. Not having enough sex with your husband. General disagreeableness." His beady eyes bore into my soul. "Not living every day like it's your last."

I have a problem with authority, but I am sheepish. Especially about the sex. "Consider this a warning," the chicken says. He disappears in a cloud of red smoke.

I am released from the hospital. Everyone tells me I am lucky to be alive.

I try to change. When my kids dump hand cream on the floor to make a slip 'n slide, I just laugh and squeeze the little moppets. When I have sex with my husband, I make a point of not looking at the clock. When I stand in line at the post office, I don't glare at the old lady in front paying in nickels and dimes. I think back to the mountaintop. I Count My Blessings.

But living every day like it's my last is tiring. There's work and a broken furnace and the school carnival and a weird stain on the counter. The car needs an oil change. I'm so frazzled I go to the store for baby food and accidentally shoplift a ham. What I'm trying to say is, I stop Savoring The Precious Moments.

"You AGAIN?" God thunders, flames shooting from his cock's comb.

I am back on the mountaintop. My body lies in the street below, where I have just been hit by a teen-age driver. The girl wears a marching band uniform and cries softly into her epaulette.

God emits a blast of heat. "Are you some kind of dumb? How many lessons in gratitude do you need?"

The smell of sulfur makes me cough. "It's just, ahem, I have a lot going on right now..." I don't tell Him how I felt when I snapped at my kids. Embarrassed, yes, but also relieved, like I popped the seam of a too-tight dress.

"I gifted you life, and I can take it away. You have one more chance. Next time..." He takes a claw and makes a slashing motion across His neck.

Like I said, I have a problem with authority. "This is a con," I mutter. How is it a "gift" if there are strings attached?

The chicken raises his wings. "No BACKTALK!" A gust of wind knocks me into a cloud.

I squint through the puffs of mist. I straighten. "It's my life. I can be busy if I want. Ungrateful." I don't even mention the ham, which I have no intention of returning.

He beats his wings. The wind rises with a howl. "You can't force a person to Live For Today!" I yell as a whirlwind sweeps me up and casts me from the mountain.

Spinning, I know I will spend the rest of my life avoiding open water. Checking seatbelts. Sniffing the potato salad at picnics. I know I am a marked woman.

From the sky my body looks like a pat of flesh on the asphalt. I hurtle towards it.

earthling

I think Bree Nicholson suspects. Why else would she look at me like that? First period English, Mr. Carmichael asked me to name themes in *Our Town*. I started talking about the transient quality of human existence and saw her mouth drop open. Her glossy bottom lip was as flaccid as taffy. She nudged Tommy Gardner and said, loudly enough for the whole class to hear, "Rhea Diarrhea is a freakazoid."

My instructions are to fit in. At least, I think so—I never got this in writing, and my memory isn't what it used to be. I can't even remember how to contact the Boss. So I stood in front of the class and kept talking about Wilder's rendering of temporal instability and the universal need for connection, all while trying to keep my left eye from twitching. That's something that seems to attract unwanted attention. That and the scars.

I'm an imposter. I try to act natural, but things don't come out right; I don't even know what acting "natural" means anymore. At lunch I hover outside myself as the other kids gossip and laugh and give each other wedgies. After school I do calc problems and look out the window. The sky is gray and impenetrable, a curtain pulled shut. I'm here for a reason; I can't remember what it is, but I know I'm not qualified.

Dave and Phyllis are the parents I've been assigned. It's easy to pretend with them. I eat the meat loaf they put in front of me. I do the dishes.

They ask if I've finished my homework, and I say yes. They ask about my day, then turn on the TV before I can answer.

Tonight it's *E.T.* A stranded alien hooks up a toy computer to some wires, attaches an umbrella, and puts a call in to outer space. The moment he connects, I sit straight up. I remember something.

I wait for Dave and Phyllis to go to bed. Then I rummage through drawers until I find a cassette player, a telephone cord, and a jack-in-the-box. I scotch-tape everything together and run outside. The stars twinkle like lights on an airport runway. I hit Play and call the Boss. "Sir?"

The cassette player hums.

"Requesting permission to cancel this mission, sir."

"Rhea." His voice is a bell in the night. "Have you accomplished your objective?"

"I'm not sure. Every day I forget more and more." I close my eyes and realize I'm crying. "Please let me come home."

"You aborted your last mission."

I touch my scars, taut across my wrists.

"You squandered precious resources."

I push Stop. But not before the Boss, light-years away, transmits final instructions: "Stay until this mission is complete. Until you leave behind more than you brought."

Somewhere a trout gasps for breath on a stream bank. Its jeweled scales glitter in the moonlight.

I watch the sky until orange bleeds into black. Then I go inside and get ready for school.

acknowledgements

These stories originally appeared in the following publications, to which I make grateful acknowledgement here:

New Delta Review, "Hereafter"
The Pinch, "Self-Reflection"
Entropy, "Cain, Knocking"
TSR: The Southampton Review Online, "Parcel Post"
Lost Balloon, "Corner of My Eye"
The Cincinnati Review miCRo, "Earthling"

9 781736 947760